www.kindermusik.com

ISBN 1-58987-112-X

Published in 2005 by Kindermusik International, Inc.

Library of Congress Cataloging-in-Publication Data
Simon, Charnan.
  Tressa the musical princess / by Charnan Simon ; illustrated by Joy Allen.
      p. cm.
  Summary: Tressa, who is sure she is a princess, spends her time practicing important princess
skills and hoping for an opportunity to save the day, and when her baby brother provides the
chance, she finds just the right magic.
  ISBN 1-58987-112-X (hardcover)
  [1. Princesses—Fiction. 2. Babies—Fiction. 3. Brothers and sisters—Fiction. 4. Family life—Fiction.]
I. Allen, Joy, ill. II. Title.
  PZ7.S6035Tr 2005
  [Fic]—dc22
                                                                                        2005007787

Do-Re-Me & You! is a trademark of Kindermusik International, Inc.

Printed in China
First Printing, March 2005

Tressa
the Musical Princess

by
Charnan Simon

illustrated by
Joy Allen

Tressa MacDonald was sure that she was a princess.

"Maybe I was left on our doorstep by a wrinkled crone who was really a fairy godmother in disguise," she told her dog, Archie.

"Probably Mom and Dad are the queen and king of a faraway land, who were banished by the spell of a wicked witch," she told her cat, Chester.

"Perhaps one day you'll grow up to be a prince," she told her baby brother, Jack, doubtfully.

4

Princess Tressa led a busy life. She consulted with her Royal Advisors on matters great and small.

5

She graciously granted audiences to
her admiring subjects.

6

She practiced important princess skills—escaping from enchanted towers, fending off fire-breathing dragons, and galloping to the rescue on Lady Elinor, her royal snow-white steed.

9

It wasn't always easy being a princess. Enchanted spells, for instance, often went wrong.

"Tressa!" said her mother. "Please watch what you're doing! You nearly knocked over your milk!"

Tressa sighed and looked at her wand. "You're supposed to turn things into chocolate," she scolded.

Then there was the matter of chores.

"Say, Tressa," called her father. "Want to give me a hand with these leaves?"

"No, thank you," said Tressa. "Princesses don't rake." Then, taking another look at her father's surprised face, she changed her mind. "Well, maybe just this once."

13

And baby Jack could be, well, a monster. "Jack!" Tressa was always shrieking. "You're eating my wand!"

Still, Tressa never lost hope that somehow, someway, Princess Tressa would save the day. Every night after her parents tucked her in bed, she sang herself to sleep with her own special princess song:

Lady Princess, strong and true,
Whispering this song to you—
Enchantment comes in many ways:
Flowers, fancies, sunlit days,
Moonbeam nights when fairies play . . .
But hush now, Princess. Sleep! I say.

15

One day, baby Jack was being especially awful.

"He's teething," said Mom with a sigh. "It's making him a little cranky."

A little cranky! Tressa had never seen such a grumpy baby. Jack squawked when they pushed him to the park in his stroller. He crabbed when they fed him mushy peaches and peas for his lunch. And when they tried to put him down for his afternoon nap, Jack roared like an angry dragon.

16

"I'll say one thing for you, Jack,"
Tressa's father said over the din. "You've
got a monster set of lungs!"

"Teething is hard on babies, but I don't remember Tressa ever being quite this unhappy." Even her mother was beginning to sound frazzled. "Will you watch him while I warm up a bottle, Tressa?"

Tressa looked long and hard at baby Jack. "It is time for Princess Tressa to put a spell on the monster dragon who has invaded her kingdom," she said aloud, and she waved her enchanted wand over Jack's scrunched-up, howling face.

Jack paused in his angry crying when he felt the silky ribbons brush his cheeks. He gulped and hiccupped and blinked his eyes as he watched the glittering rod wave gently over his face. He gave the tiniest hint of a smile and said "Gorra!" as he raised one fat baby hand to reach for the magic wand.

Tressa let Jack grab a tiny fistful of
ribbons and rub them against his cheek.
Then, softer than soft, she began to sing
her own special bedtime song, with just
a few princely changes:

Monster dragon, listen, do,
As I put my spell on you—
Enchantment comes in many ways:
Rattles, castles, treasured days,
Dream-filled nights where heroes play . . .
But hush now, Young Prince. Sleep! I say.

Slowly, surely, sweetly, Jack's eyes
began to close and his breathing grew
peaceful and quiet. His baby fist relaxed
as Tressa kept singing, and the enchanted
ribbons soon lay in a crumpled heap on
the blankets.

"Tressa!" Her mother and father had tiptoed into the room and were whispering, amazed, at the sound-asleep baby. "You wonder, you! However did you do it? You've saved the day!"

Tressa just nodded—kindly, graciously, royally—and went on singing. She was Princess Tressa, of course, and saving the day was what princesses did best.